For Grandmas and Grandads everywhere,
and for all their grandchildren.

Special thanks to Kristina Petersen for her multi-lingual Santa mail, and to Mum for last-minute proof-reading.

First published in Great Britain in 2021 by Andersen Press Ltd.,

20 Vauxhall Bridge Road, London SW1V 2SA, UK

Vijverlaan 48, 3062 HL Rotterdam, Nederland

Copyright © Chris Naylor-Ballesteros 2021.

The right of Chris Naylor-Ballesteros to be identified as the author and illustrator of this work has been asserted

by him in accordance with the Copyright, Designs and Patents Act, 1988.

Printed and bound in China.

1   3   5   7   9   10   8   6   4   2

British Library Cataloguing in Publication Data available. ISBN 978 1 83913 032 8

Tiny Reindeer

Chris Naylor-Ballesteros

Andersen Press

Tiny Reindeer was just like any other reindeer, but with one big difference. He was very, very tiny.

He wasn't just smaller than the others, he felt different too. And never more so than at one particular time of year...

Christmas time.

As Christmas came ever nearer, the big, stamping, snorting reindeer were busy helping Santa get ready for the most important night of the year.

"Ho! Ho! Ho! Let's get to it, there are jobs to be done!" boomed Santa, as he fed his herd.

"Ho… ho… humph," sighed Tiny Reindeer. "I wish there was a job I could do, even just a *tiny* one."

Every year Tiny Reindeer tried
very hard to find a way to help,
but whatever he did went wrong.
He got tangled in the reins
and harnesses.

He fell into the water bowls.

And he had to be rescued
from the sticky tape when he
tried to wrap the presents.

On the day before Christmas Eve, Santa spoke to Tiny Reindeer. "Why don't you have a look in the Post Room? You might be able to help there," he suggested, kindly. "There's one last little pile of children's letters to sort."
Tiny Reindeer wasn't so sure.

A *little* pile? Tiny ended up squashed under an enormous mess of mixed-up Christmas letters. But as he struggled to wriggle free, a letter with a reindeer drawn on it caught his eye. It was from a little girl. "Hmm. Maybe this one's for me," he thought.

Against all the rules, Tiny sneaked it away with him to his quiet little corner of the stables and read it. And he came up with a plan.

The next morning everyone was busy getting ready for take off. And as night-time fell Santa took the reins of his magnificent sleigh, harnessing the puffing reindeer ready for the long journey ahead.

Nobody noticed a tiny
passenger leaping into a hiding place
on the back of Santa's sleigh – a secret voyager on a special mission.

Throughout the long and snowy night Santa's sleigh flew across the sky, crossing oceans and covering continents.

Tiny Reindeer stayed hidden until finally the moment he'd waited for had arrived.

He took a deep breath and leapt from the sleigh into the freezing air as Santa and his galloping herd disappeared into the darkness.

From a bag on Tiny Reindeer's back ballooned a
perfectly sized paper parachute, made from the
little girl's letter. He aimed for the chimney pot on top
of one particular house, and...

Whoosh...

He plunged through the hole, tumbling into the fireplace below.

Climbing out he tiptoed towards an open door,

which led to a hallway   and an enormous staircase.

"Oh no," thought Tiny Reindeer. The stairs were far too big for him. Tired and cold, he couldn't climb the first one, let alone all the others. And he didn't even know if he had landed in the right house. As he lowered his head and tears came to his eyes, Tiny Reindeer began to wonder if he'd made a very big mistake.

Suddenly there was a noise in the room behind him, a crash and a bash, a huffing and a puffing, then footsteps moving across the floor. Tiny Reindeer tried to hide in the shadows, keeping quiet and still.

But a huge figure stepped into the hallway and looked straight down at him…

Santa!

"Good job I was keeping an eye on you, Tiny Reindeer,"
he whispered. "It looks like you could do with some help."

Santa carefully took off the paper parachute and folded it into his coat pocket. Then, dusting off the soot and dirt, he carried Tiny Reindeer upstairs to a bedroom where a little girl was fast asleep. A beautiful, tiny wooden sleigh sat right beside her.

She didn't hear the door open, nor did she see Santa tiptoe across the floor. She didn't even stir when Tiny Reindeer leapt softly on to her pillow.

"Goodbye, my little friend. I must be on my way," Santa whispered. "I'll try to drop in and see you next year."

And then he was gone.

Tiny Reindeer settled down, warm and cosy on the pillow. Exhausted after his adventure, he wondered what Christmas morning might bring, until eventually he yawned and closed his eyes.

The little girl remained fast asleep, dreaming excitedly of a tiny sleigh and...

"A tiny reindeer! *My* tiny reindeer!" she cried out when she woke on Christmas morning. Tiny stood proudly on the little girl's hands and knew he had finally found where he belonged – and with the most beautiful sleigh he'd ever seen, handmade to fit him perfectly.

His plan had worked...

with just a tiny bit of help from Santa.